Isaac Brock

The Battle of Queenston Heights

Anatiposi

Isaac Brock

The Battle of Queenston Heights

Reprint of the original.

1st Edition 2023 | ISBN: 978-3-38230-546-8

Anatiposi Verlag is an imprint of Outlook Verlagsgesellschaft mbH.

Verlag (Publisher): Outlook Verlag GmbH, Zeilweg 44, 60439 Frankfurt, Deutschland
Vertretungsberechtigt (Authorized to represent): E. Roepke, Zeilweg 44, 60439 Frankfurt, Deutschland
Druck (Print): Books on Demand GmbH, In de Tarpen 42, 22848 Norderstedt, Deutschland

THE BATTLE

OF

QUEENSTON HEIGHTS:

BEING A NARRATIVE OF THE

OPENING OF THE WAR OF 1812,

WITH NOTICES OF THE LIFE OF

MAJOR-GENERAL
SIR ISAAC BROCK, K.B.,

AND DESCRIPTION OF

THE MONUMENT ERECTED TO HIS MEMORY.

EDITED BY JOHN SYMONS, ESQ.

TORONTO:
THOMPSON & CO., PRINTERS, 77 KING STREET EAST.

1859.

SOUTH WEST VIEW, OF THE

BROCK MONUMENT,

ERECTED ON QUEENSTON HEIGHTS,
1856.

TO

THE MILITIA,

INDIAN WARRIORS,

AND

PEOPLE

OF UPPER CANADA,

By whose loyalty and liberality, aided by the untiring exertions, judgment
and good taste of

THE BUILDING COMMITTEE,

This splendid tribute of a country's gratitude has been erected,

THIS LITTLE WORK

IS

RESPECTFULLY INSCRIBED

BY

THE AUTHOR.

Toronto, September, 1859.

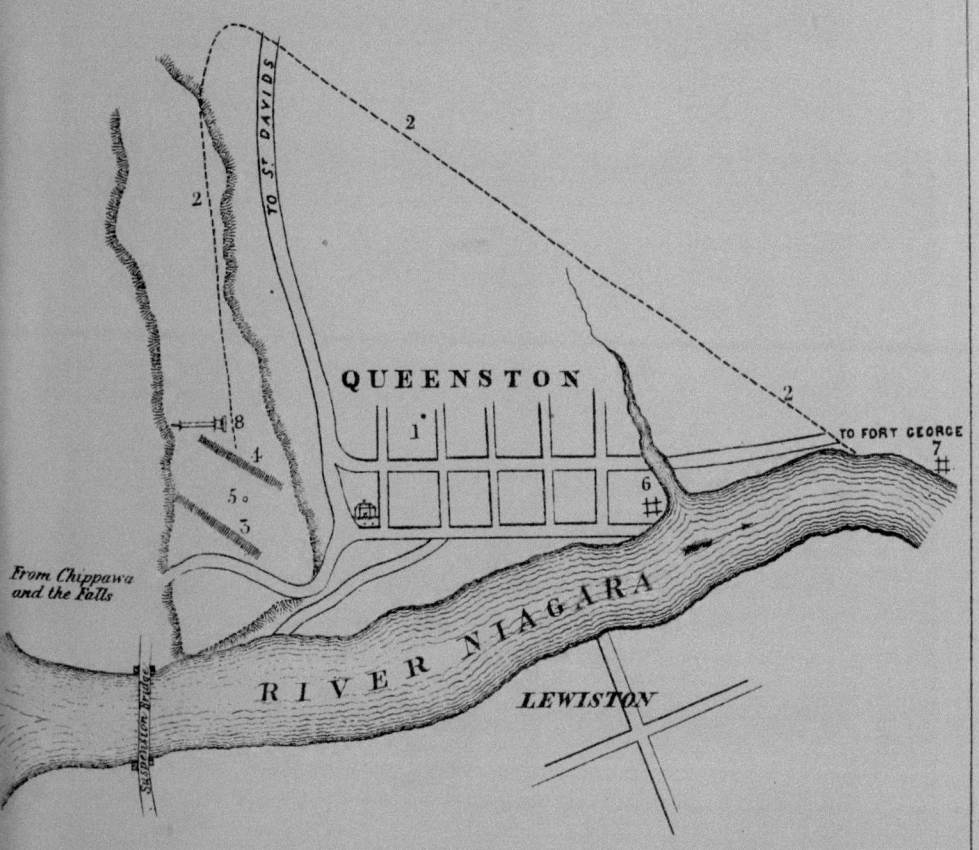

PLAN OF THE BATTLE OF QUEENSTON.

QUEENSTON

TO ST DAVIDS

TO FORT GEORGE

From Chippawa
and the Falls

RIVER NIAGARA

LEWISTON

1. Spot where Brock fell
2. Road by which the reinforcements from Fort George gained the Heights in the afternoon
3. American line as drawn up in afternoon
4. British line   do.   do.
5. Site of first monument
6. Old Fort
7. Vromont's Battery
8. Brock's monument

John Ellis Lith. Toronto.

THE BATTLE OF QUEENSTON HEIGHTS.

On the 13th October, 1812, was fought the Battle of Queenston Heights.

We desire to tread lightly upon the ground of the quarrel between Great Britain and the United States. We had been almost disposed to pass over entirely this dark era in the history of the two nations, least an allusion to it might, in the remotest degree, disturb that friendly feeling which now happily exists between them, but our history would not be complete if we did so ; we shall, however, only place on record, a few general notices of the events which preceded and accompanied this war : landmarks, which may guide the reader to the clear comprehension of the subject which is the immediate object of these pages. We shall endeavour to be truthful and exact in every statement, drawing our information from official documents, and historical volumns, and in not a few instances from parties themselves who were present on the field of action. And if the reflections which our subject may occasionally suggest do not carry conviction to the minds of some, we hope for that forbearance which we should ourselves be inclined to show, were this little work compiled by one whose sympathies were opposite to our own.

It was manifest from the temper shewn by the President and Congress of the United States, towards the close of the year 1811, that nothing could prevent a war between that country and Great Britain, but either a change in the system pursued by the latter, or a dread in the former to come to the point of actual hostilities, under the prospect of much suffering from abroad and much discontent at home. When it was seen that the resolutions of the Committee of Foreign Relations were all carried by great majorities, of which the lowest was 109 to 22 and the highest 110 to 11, and when a motion in the House of Representatives for the indefinite postponement of a bill for raising 25,000 additional troops was rejected by a majority of 98 to 29, it was evident that hostile proceedings were

A

nearly determined on.   At this time the advocates of war, besides the lure of rich prizes to be made by the American privateers, threw out confident expectations of the conquest of Canada.

Mr. Gallatin's budget was laid before Congress on January 12th, 1812. It recommended a loan of $10,000,000 to meet the exigencies of that year, and calculated that a like loan would be necessary for several years to come. It also gave the comfortable prospect of continually increasing taxes to pay the interest of these loans.   But when the particulars of raising these necessary supplies for the war and equipping an adequate military force came to be discussed in Congress, the great majorities in favor of the measures proposed by Government, no longer appeared, and several questions were barely carried.

It would be superfluous to give a sketch of the arguments used on each side in this discussion; arguments referring to the beaten topic of the French decrees and English orders in Council regarding neutral commerce and the right of search, and which proved totally inefficacious to produce conviction on the minds of the different parties.   In this unhappy quarrel both parties in England and the United States boasted of their moderation and forbearance, both alleged the reason and justice of their cause, yet both were, in fact, determined by motives of state policy operating exclusively upon themselves.

The temper of the House of Representatives with respect to a war with England, was rendered manifest by the result of a motion by Mr. Randolph, on May 29th.   That gentleman, after a long speech, condemning the present relations of the United States with Great Britain and France, submitted to the House the following resolution : "That under the present circumstances it is inexpedient to resort to a war with Great Britain." The question being put that the House do proceed to the consideration of the said resolution, it was negatived by 62 votes against 37.   All hopes of pacific measures now, therefore, rested upon the determination of the Senate.   On June 4th, the President laid before Congress copies of a correspondence which had lately taken place between Mr. Foster and Mr. Monroe.   It chiefly consisted of a long argumentative letter from the former relative to the old subject of the orders in Council and the French decrees, of which it is sufficient to remark that not the least expectation is held forth of any further relaxation on the part of Great Britain.   On the contrary, Mr. F. says expressively, "America, as the case now stands, has not a pretence for claiming from Great Britain a repeal of her orders in Council." Previously, however, to this communication, the President had sent a long message to both Houses, dated June 1st, in which he sets forth all the injuries and hostile measures (as he considered them) practiced by the Government of Great Britain and still persisted in towards the United States, and recommended the subject to their early deliberations. In consequence, discussions with closed doors took place in the two houses, the final result of which was, an act passed on June 18th, declaring *the actual existence of war* between the United Kingdom of Great Britain and Ireland and the United States of America. The majority in the House of Representatives on this momentous occasion for declaring war was 79 against 49. The supporters of war were chiefly the southern and western states to Pennsylvania inclusive; the votes for peace were chiefly in the eastern and northern states, New York taking the lead. As commercial grievances constituted a great part of the complaints against Great Britain adduced to justify the resort to arms, it is highly probably that if the orders in Council had been repealed early enough for intelligence of the event to have reached America before the final decision, the advocates for peace would have acquired so much additional strength as at least to have deferred the declaration of hostilities till time had been given for negotiating on the other points in dispute. In England little doubt seemed to be entertained that the news of the repeal of the orders in Council would arrive time enough to prevent actual war.* She had but recently stated that America had no pretence for claiming the repeal of these orders, yet for the sake of peace she repealed them. That was not the time for her to engage in another war, and least of all in a war with her own child.

Besides England had many obvious reasons for endeavoring to avert the calamities of an American war at that period. She was engaged in a very arduous contest in Europe, she had the most numerous and formidable enemies to contend with, she had the interest of her commerce to maintain, which is always dependent in some degree on a friendly connection with America; and she had, moreover, a natural and generous aversion to conquer before she could bring herself to draw the sword against a a people connected with her by a resemblance of language, laws and insti-

---

*The United States declared war on 18th June, the revocation of the Orders in Council took place on 17th June. Had the Atlantic Telegraph been then in operation a disastrous war might have been avoided.

tutions. These were motives sufficiently powerful to have restrained English Ministers even if they had not been otherwise remarkable for mildness and forbearance.

But unfortunately the news of the repeal of these orders in Council came too late, and having hastily rushed into war it was difficult for America to recede; indeed subsequent events rendered it highly probable that the American Government of that day had anticipated credit from the commencement of the war, especially from the conquest of Canada, which seems to have been regarded as an easy task.

Several acts of hostility occurred between the two powers, attended with various success, but we hasten to the beginning of the campaign against Canada.

The first exploits of the American army, though such as might naturally have been expected, from the total want of preparation on the part of their government or people for a war, were, nevertheless very different from what the democratic party who had driven the nation into it, had anticipated. Early in July, General Hull invaded Upper Canada with a force of five thousand eight hundred men, having crossed the St. Lawrence at Detroit, and marched to Sandwich; he there issued a Proclamation in which he expressed entire confidence of success. "I come prepared" he said, "for every contingency. I have a force which will look down all opposition, and that force is but the vanguard of a much greater." He then directed his operations against Fort Amherstburg, but he was repulsed in three different attempts to cross the River Canard, on which it stands, and General Brock having collected a force of seven hundred British regulars and militia, and six hundred auxiliary Indians, not only relieved that Fort, but compelled Hull to retire to Fort Detroit, where he was soon after invested by General Brock. Batteries having been constructed and a fire opened, preparations were made for an assault, and after the town had been cannonaded for two or three hours, on the 15th and 16th of August, the American Commander surrendered himself and his Army of two thousand five hundred men, and thirty-three pieces of cannon; a proud trophy to have been taken with the Fort of Detroit by a British force of no more than seven hundred men, including militia and six hundred auxiliary Indians.

At the same time a small British force had summoned and taken the American Fort at Mackinac. These successes had the most powerful effect in increasing the spirit and energy of the militia of Upper Canada, the inhabitants of which, of British origin, and strongly animated with patriotic and national feelings, had taken up arms universally, to repel the hated invasion of their republican neighbours. An armistice was soon after agreed to between Sir George Prevost, the British Governor of Canada, and General Dearborn, the American Commander-in-Chief on the northern frontier, in the hope that the repeal of the orders in Council, would, by removing the only real ground of quarrel between the two countries, have led to a termination of hostilities. But in this hope, however reasonable soever, they were disappointed ; the American Government, impelled by the Democratic constituencies, had not yet abandoned their visions of Canadian conquest, and they not only disavowed the armistice, but determined upon a vigorous prosecution of the contest. As this determination unveiled the real motives which had led to the war, and demonstrated that the orders in Council had been a mere pretext, it gave rise to the most violent dissatisfaction in the northern Provinces of the union, who were likely from their dependance upon British commerce to be the greatest sufferers by the contest. So far did this proceed that many memorials were addressed to the President from these States, in which they set forth that they contemplated with abhorrence an alliance with the then Emperor of France, every action of whose life had been an attempt to effect the extinction of all vestiges of freedom—that the repeal of the orders in Council had removed the only legitimate object of complaint against the British Government, and that if any attempts were made to introduce French troops into the United States, they would regard them as enemies. The most remarkable of these memorials were from Rockingham, in New Hampshire, and from thirty-four cities and counties of the State of New York. Connecticut and Massachusetts openly refused to send their contingents, or to impose the taxes which had been voted by Congress.*

The American Government, however, were no-ways intimidated, either by the bad success of their arms in Canada, or by the menaces of the northern Provinces of the Union. Later in the season they assembled on the Niagara frontier, a force of six thousand three hundred men ; of this force, three thousand one hundred and seventy (nine hundred of whom were regular troops,) were at Lewiston under the command of General

*Ann. Reg., 1812.

Van Rensselaer. In the American reports this army is set down as eight thousand strong, with fifteen pieces of field ordnance.

To oppose this force, Major-General Brock had part of the 41st and 49th Regiments, a few companies of Militia, and about two hundred Indians, in all fifteen hundred men; but so dispersed in different posts, at and between Fort Erie and Fort George, that only a small number was available at any one point.

Before daylight on the morning of the 13th of October, a large division of General Van Rensselaer's army, numbering between thirteen and fourteen hundred, under Brigadier-General Wadsworth, effected a landing at the lower end of the Village of Queenston, (opposite Lewiston) and made an attack upon the position which was defended with the utmost determined bravery by the two flank companies of the 49th Regiment, commanded by Captains Dennis and Williams, aided by such of the militia forces and Indians as could be collected in the vicinity. Captain Dennis marched his Company to the landing place opposite Lewiston, and was soon followed by the Light Company of the 49th, and the few militia who could be hastily assembled. Here the attempt of the enemy to effect a passage, was, for some time successfully resisted, and several boats were either disabled or sunk by the fire from the one-gun battery on the heights and that from the masked battery, about a mile below. Several boats were, by the fire from this last battery, so annoyed, that falling below the landing place, they were compelled to drop down with the current and recross to the American side. A considerable force, however, had effected a landing some distance above, and succeeded in gaining the summit of the mountain. No resistance could now be offered to the crossing from Lewiston, except by the battery at Vromont's Point, half a mile below, and from this a steady and harassing fire was kept up, which did considerable execution.

At this juncture Sir Isaac Brock arrived. He had for some days suspected this invasion, and on the preceding evening he called his staff together and gave to each the necessary instructions. Agreeably to his usual custom he rose before day light, and hearing the cannonade, awoke Major Glegg, and called for his horse Alfred, which Sir James Craig had presented to him. He then gallopped eagerly from Fort George to the scene of action, and with his two aides-de-camp passed up the hill at full gallop in front of the light company, under a heavy fire of the artillery and musketry from the American shore. On reaching the 18-pounder battery at the top of the hill, they dismounted and took a view of passing events, which at that moment appeared highly favorable. But in a few minutes a firing was heard, which proceeded from a strong detachment of American regulars under Captain Wool, who, as just stated, had succeeded in gaining the brow of the heights in rear of the battery, by a fisherman's path up the rocks, which being reported as impassable, was not guarded. Sir Isaac Brock and his aides-de-camp had not even time to remount, but were obliged to retire precipitately with the twelve men stationed in the battery, which was quickly occupied by the enemy. Capt. Wool having sent forward about 150 regulars, Capt. William's detachment of about 100 men advanced to meet them, personally directed by the General, who, observing the enemy to waver, ordered a charge, which was promptly executed ; but as the Americans gave way the result was not equal to his expectations. Capt. Wool sent a re-inforcement to his regulars, but notwithstanding which, the whole were driven to the edge of the bank.* Here some of the American Officers were on the point of hoisting a white flag with an intention to surrender, when Capt. Wool tore it off and re-animated his dispirited troops. They now opened a heavy fire of musketry, and conspicuous from his dress, his height, and the enthusiasm with which he animated his little band, the British Commander was soon singled out, and he fell about an hour after his arrival.

The fatal bullet entered his right breast, and passed through his left side. He had but that instant said, " Push on the York Volunteers !" and he lived only long enough to request that his fall might not be noticed, or prevent the advance of his brave troops ; adding a wish which could not be distinctly understood, that some token of remembrance should be transmitted to his sister. He died unmarried, and on the same day, a week previously, he had completed his forty-third year. The lifeless corpse was immediately conveyed into a house close by, where it remained until the afternoon, unperceived by the enemy. His Provincial Aid-de-camp, Lieutenant-Colonel McDonell of the militia, and the Attorney General of Upper Canada, a fine promising young man, was mortally wounded soon after his chief, and died the next day, at the early age of twenty-five years. Although one bullet had passed through his body, and he was wounded in four places, yet he survived twenty

---

*Capt. Wool's letter to Col. Van Rensselaer, 23rd October, 1812.

hours, and during a period of excruciating agony his thoughts and words were constantly occupied with lamentations for his deceased commander and friend. He fell while gallantly charging up the hill with 190 men, chiefly of the York Volunteers, by which charge the enemy was compelled to spike the 18-pounder, in the battery there.*

Captain Wool in his despatch to Colonel Van Rensselaer describes this affair as follows: " In pursuance of your order, we proceeded round the point and ascended the rocks, which brought us partly in rear of the battery. We took it without much resistance. I immediately formed the troops in rear of the battery and fronting the village, when I observed General Brock with his troops formed, consisting of four [only two] companies of the 49th regiment, and a few militia, marching for our left flank. I immediately detached a party of one hundred and fifty men to take possession of the heights above Queenston battery, and to hold Gen. Brock in check; but in consequence of his superior force they retreated. I sent a re-inforcement, notwithstanding which, the enemy drove us to the edge of the bank, when, with the greatest exertions, we brought the troops to a stand, and ordered the officers to bring their men to a charge as soon as the ammunition was expended, which was executed with some confusion, and in a few moments the enemy retreated. We pursued them to the edge of the heights when Colonel McDonell had his horse shot from under him, and himself was mortally wounded. In the interim, General Brock, in attempting to rally his forces was killed, when the enemy dispersed in every direction."

The troops who now retreated, formed in front of Vromont's Battery, and there awaited re-inforcements, while General Van Rensselaer, considering the victory complete, crossed over in order to give directions about fortifying the camp, which he intended to occupy on the British Territory, and then re-crossed to hasten the sending over re-inforcements.

Early in the afternoon, a body of about fifty Mohawks, under Norton and young Brant, advanced through the woods, took up a position in front, and a very sharp skirmish ensued, which ended in the Indians retiring on the re-inforcements which had now begun to arrive from Fort George. The re-inforcement consisted of three hundred and eighty rank and file of the 41st regiment, and Captains Jarvis,' Crook's and

---

* Tupper's life of Brock.

McEwan's flank companies of the 1st Lincoln; Captains Nellis' and W. Crook's flank companies of the 4th Lincoln; Hall's, Durand's, and Applegarth's companies of the 5th Lincoln; Cameron's, Heward's, and Chisholm's flank companies of the York Militia; Major Merritt's yeomanry corps, and a body of Swayzee's militia artillery. A short time afterwards, Colonel Clark of the militia arrived from Chippewa, with Captain Bullock's company of the 41st; Captain R. Hamilton and Row's flank companies of the 2d Lincoln and volunteer militia; and many persons who were both by their situations in life and by their advanced age exempt from serving in the militia, made common cause—they seized their arms and flew to the field of action.

Judge Clench, of Niagara, an old half-pay officer from His Majesty's service, who had retired from the command of the 1st Lincoln Militia, in company with a few others exempt from service, with a truly patriotic zeal followed their beloved general from Fort George to Queenston, and ranged themselves in the ranks as volunteers to drive the enemy from their shore.

At this time, about two in the afternoon, the whole British and Indian force thus assembled was about 1000 men, of whom 600 were regulars. In numbers the Americans were about equal—courage they had, but they wanted the confidence and discipline of British soldiers.

After carefully reconnoitering, Gen. Sheaffe, who had arrived from Fort George, and who had now assumed the command, commenced the attack by an advance of his left flank, composed of the light company of the 41st under Lieutenant McIntyre, supported by a body of Militia and Indians. After a volley the bayonet was resorted to and the American's right driven in. The main body now advanced under cover of the fire from the two three pounders, and after a short conflict forced the Americans over the first ridge of the heights to the road leading from Queenston to the Falls. The fight was maintained on both sides with courage truly heroic. The British regulars and militia charged in rapid succession until they succeeded in turning the left flank of their column which rested on the summit of the hill. The Americans who attempted to escape into the woods were quickly driven back by the Indians, and many cut off in their return to the main body, and terrified at the sight of these exasperated warriors, flung themselves wildly over the cliffs, and endeavoured to cling to the bushes which grew upon them; but some losing their hold

B

were dashed frightfully on the rocks beneath ; while others who reached
the river, perished in their attempts to swim across it.   The event of the
day no longer appeared doubtful.

Major-General Van Rensselaer, commanding the American army, per-
ceiving his reinforcements embarking very slowly, re-crossed the river to
accelerate their movements ; but to his utter astonishment he found that
at the very moment when their services were most required, the ardor of
the unengaged troops had entirely subsided. General Van Rensselaer rode
in all directions through the camp urging his men by every consideration
to pass over.   Lieutenant-Colonel Bloome, who had been wounded in the
action and re-crossed the river, together with Judge Peck who happened
to be in Lewiston at the time, mounted their horses and rode through the
camp, exhorting the companies to proceed but all in vain.* Crowds of
the United States militia remained on the American bank of the river to
which they had not been marched in any order, but ran as a mob : not
one of them would cross.   They had seen the wounded re-crossing ; they
had seen the Indians ; and they had seen the "green tigers," as they
called the 49th from their green facings, and were panic struck.   There
were those to be found in the American ranks who, at this critical juncture could talk of the Constitution and the right of the militia to refuse
crossing the imaginary line which separates the two countries.†

General Van Rensselaer having found that it was impossible to urge a
a single man to cross the river to reinforce the army on the heights, and
that army having nearly expended its ammunition, boats were immediately
sent to cover their retreat ; but a desultory fire which was maintained upon the ferry from a battery on the bank at the lower end of Queenston,
completely dispersed the boats, and many of the boatmen re-landed and
fled in dismay.   Brigadier-General Wadsworth was, therefore, compelled,
after a vigorous conflict had been maintained for some time upon both
sides, to surrender himself and all his officers and nine hundred men, between three and four o'clock in the afternoon.

The loss of the British army was sixteen killed and sixty-nine
wounded ; while that on the side of the Americans was not less than
nine hundred men made prisoners and one gun and two colors taken, and
ninety killed and about one hundred wounded.   But amongst the

---

*Major-General Van Rensselaer's letter to Major-General M. Dearborn, dated
Head Quarters, Lewiston, 14th October, 1812.
†American Report of the Battle of Queenston.

killed of the British army the Government and the country had to deplore the loss of one of their bravest and most zealous generals in Sir Isaac Brock, and one whose memory will long live in the warmest affections of every Canadian and British subject, and the country had also to deplore the loss of the eminent services and talents of Lieutenant-Colonel McDonell, Provincial Aid-de-Camp and Attorney General of the Province, whose gallantry and merit rendered him worthy of his chief.

Captains Dennis and Williams, commanding the flank companies of the 49th regiment which were stationed at Queenston were wounded, bravely contending at the head of their men against superior numbers. Captain Dennis, though with great pain and difficulty, kept the field to the last. Great praise was due to Captain Holcroft of the royal artillery, for his judicious and skilful co-operation with the guns and howitzers under his immediate superintendence, the well-directed fire from which contributed materially to the fortunate result of the day. Captain Derenzy of the 41st regiment brought up the reinforcement of that corps from Fort George, and Captain Bullock led that of the same regiment from Chippawa, and under their command those detachments acquitted themselves in such a manner as to sustain the reputation which the 41st regiment had already acquired in the vicinity of Detroit.

Major-General Brock, soon after his arrival at Queenston, had sent down orders for battering the American Fort Niagara. Brigadier-Major Evans who was left in charge of Fort George, directed the operations against it with so much effect as to silence its fire, and to force the troops to abandon it, and by his prudent precautions he prevented mischief of a most serious nature which otherwise might have been effected, the enemy having used heated shot in firing at Fort George. In these services he was most effectually aided by Colonel Claus, (who remained in the Fort at the desire of Major-General Sheaffe,) and by Captain Vigoureux of the Royal Engineers. The guns on Fort George were under the immediate direction of Captains Powell and Cameron of the militia artillery.

Lieutenant Crowther of the 41st regiment had charge of two three-pounders which had accompanied the little corps, and they were employed with very good effect.

Captain Glegg of the 49th regiment, Aid-de-camp to General Brock, afforded most essential assistance, and the services of Lieutenant Fowler of the 41st regiment, Assistant Deputy Quarter Master General, were very useful. Much aid was derived too from the activity and intelligence of Lieutenant Kerr of the Glengarry Fencibles, who was employed in communications with the Indians and other flanking parties.

Lieutenant Colonels Butler and Clark of the militia, and Captains Hatt, Durand, Rowe, Applegarth, James Crooks, Cooper, Robt. Hamilton, McEwan, and Duncan Cameron, and Lieutenants Robinson and Thomas Butler, commanding flank companies of the Lincoln and York militia, led their men into action with great spirit. Major Merritt, commanding the Niagara Dragoons, gave great assistance with part of his corps; Captain A. Hamilton, belonging to it, was disabled from riding, and attached himself to the guns under Captain Holcroft, and his activity and usefulness were highly spoken of. Volunteers Shaw, Thomson, and Jarvis, attached to the flank companies of the 49th regiment, conducted themselves with great spirit; the first was wounded, and the last taken prisoner. Norton was wounded, but not badly; he and the Indians particularly distinguished themselves, and they behaved with the same bravery and humanity as they displayed at the taking of Detroit, when General Brock in the despatch to Sir George Provost, of the 17th August, 1812, says :—" They were led yesterday by Colonel Elliot and Captain McKee, and nothing could exceed their order and steadiness. A few prisoners were taken by these during the advance, whom they treated with every humanity, and it affords me much pleasure in assuring your Excellency, that such was their forbearance and attention to what was required of them, that the enemy sustained no other loss in men than was occasioned by the fire of our batteries."

In Major-General Sheaffe's despatch, which has mainly furnished the foregoing details, particular mention is made of the spirit and good conduct of His Majesty's troops of the militia, and of the other provincial corps. They were eminently conspicuous on this occasion, and this arm of the service was subsequently complimented by the Duke of Wellington, who in his protest against the third reading of the Bill to re-unite Upper and Lower Canada, stated that " The operations of the war were carried on with but little assistance from the mother country in regular troops, and had thus demonstrated that the Provinces were capable of defending themselves against all the efforts of their powerful neighbours, the United States."

Nothing could possibly exceed the heroic bravery manifested on both sides during this sanguinary contest. Colonel Van Rensselaer, Aid-de-camp to General Van Rensselaer, who led the van of the invading army, displayed much real courage in the gallant and intrepid manner in which he formed the division under his command, on the margin of the river, and led them on to the attack. He even after receiving four wounds continued to issue his orders.

Captain Wool, an officer only twenty-six years of age, likewise displayed great courage and self-devotedness to his country's service.

The names also of Brigadier-General Wadsworth, Colonel Scott, Lieutenant-Colonels Christie and Fenwick, and Captain Gibson, and several others of an inferior rank, are honorably spoken of in General Van Rensselaer's despatches to General Dearborn on the subject.

And as a tribute to the magnanimity of the enemy it is recorded, that during the movement of the funeral procession of the brave Brock from Queenston to Fort George, a distance of seven miles, minute guns were fired at every American post on that part of the lines, and even the appearance of hostilities was suspended.

Major-General Van Rensselaer also in a letter of condolence informed Major-General Sheaffe that immediately after the funeral solemnities were over on the British side, a compliment of minute guns would be paid to the hero's memory on theirs! Accordingly the cannons at Fort Niagara were fired " as a mark of respect due to a brave enemy." How much is it then to be regretted that we should ever come into collision with those who possess the same origin and the same language as ourselves, and who by their generous feelings and conduct proved that they are a liberal as they undoubtedly are a gallant people ; and may the future rivalry of both powers be, not for the unnatural destruction of each other, but for the benefit of mankind.

Major-General Sheaffe, on the morning subsequent to the battle, humanely consented to a cessation of offensive hostilities on the solicitation of Major-General Van Rensselaer, for the purpose of allowing the Americans to remove the slain and wounded.

It would be beyond the purpose of the present work to continue the history of the war. If we did so, we should have to recount how the Americans, though unsuccessful with their army in the various attacks they made on Canada, met with extraordinary and unlooked for triumphs at sea, which in Europe excited the greater sensation, that they shook the general belief that at that time prevailed of British invincibility at sea. But it must be remembered, that the great contest in the Peninsula was yet doubtful and undecided, and every sabre and bayonet that could be spared was sent to feed the army of Wellington, which rendered it a matter of impossibility to despatch any adequate force to the Canadian frontier. Whilst, therefore, we admit the gallantry which won for the Americans their laurels at sea under these peculiar and exceptional circumstances, we would at the same time express our fervent hope, not only that they may long wear them, but that two countries like Great Britain and the United States, allied by so many natural ties and secular and religious interests, may forever, as they do now, dwell together in unity and in the bonds of peace.

In sad and solemn silence were the remains of our hero conveyed from Queenston to Government House, Niagara. The body was bedewed with the tears of many affectionate friends, and after lying in state, was interred on the 16th October, with his Aid-de-Camp, at Fort George; Major Glegg, his surviving Aid-de-Camp, recollecting the decided aversion of the General to every thing that bore the appearance of ostentatious display, endeavoured to clothe the distressing ceremony with all his "native simplicity." But at the same time, there were military honors that could not be avoided, and the following was the order of the mournful procession, "of which," writes Major Glegg, "I enclose a plan; but no pen can describe the real scenes of that mournful day. A more solemn and affecting spectacle was, perhaps, never witnessed. As every arrangement connected with that affecting ceremony fell to my lot, a second attack being hourly expected, and the minds of all being fully occupied with the duties of their respective stations, I anxiously endeavoured to perform this last tribute of affection in a manner corresponding with the elevated virtues of my departed patron. Considering that an interment, in every respect military, would be the most appropriate to the character of our dear friend, I made choice of a cavalier bastion in Fort George, which his aspiring genius had lately suggested, and which had been just finished under his daily superintendance."

FORT-MAJOR CAMPBELL.
Sixty men of the 41st Regiment, commanded by a subaltern.
Sixty of the Militia, commanded by a Captain.
Two six-pounders—firing minute guns.
Remaining corps and detachments of the Garrison, with about 200 Indians
in reverse order, forming a street through which the procession passed,
extending from the Government House to the Garrison.
Band of the 41st Regiment.
Drums covered with black cloth, and muffled.
Late General's horse, fully caparisoned, led by four grooms.
Servants of the General.
The General's body Servant.

Surgeon Muirhead,	Doctor Kerr,
Doctor Moore,	Staff Surgeon Thorn.

Reverend Mr. Addison.
The body of Lieut. Colonel McDONELL, P.A.D.C.

Capt. A. Cameron,	Lieut. Jarvis,
Lieut. Robinson,	Lieut. Ridout,
J. Edwards, Esq.,	Capt. Crooks,
SUPPORTER.	SUPPORTER.
Mr. Dickson,	Capt. Cameron,

CHIEF MOURNER.
Mr. McDonell.

THE BODY OF MAJOR-GENERAL BROCK.

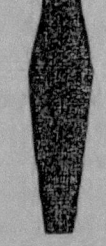

SUPPORTERS.	SUPPORTERS.
Mr. James Coffin, D.A.C.G.,	Capt. Williams, 49th Regt.,
Capt. Vigoreaux, R. E.,	Major Merritt, L.H. Lin. Mil.,
Capt. Derenzy, 41st Regt.,	Lieut. Col. Clark, Lin. Mil.,
Capt. Dennis, 49th Regt.,	Lieut. Col. Butler.,
Capt. Holcraft, R. A.	Colonel Claus.
SUPPORTER.	SUPPORTER.
Brigade Major Evans.	Capt. Glegg, A.D.C.

CHIEF MOURNERS.

Major General Sheaffe,	Lieut. Colonel Myers, D.Q.M.G.
Ensign Coffin, A.D.C.,	Lieut. Fowler, A.D.Q.M.G.

The Civil Staff.
Friends of the deceased.
Inhabitants.*

---

*Extracted from the *York Gazette*, October 24th, 1812.

The funeral solemnities on the British side being over, the touching compliment of minute guns was paid to the hero's memory on the American, to which we have already alluded.

The death of Brock occasioned universal sorrow, not only throughout Canada but in the mother country also. At the time when he assumed the government of the Province, he found a divided, disaffected, and weak people, but possessing in an eminent degree those virtues which add lustre to bravery and those talents which shine alike in the cabinet and in the field, he succeeded in gaining the full confidence of every political party, and in forming a united and strong people, capable, in their country's need, of protecting her against all the attempts of her powerful neighbours. "His manners and disposition were so conciliating," says a writer of that period, "as to gain the affection of all whom he commanded, while his innate nobleness and dignity of mind secured him a respect almost amounting to veneration."

Nature had been very bountiful to Sir Isaac Brock in those personal gifts which appear to such peculiar advantage in the army, and at the first glance the soldier and the gentleman were seen. In stature he was tall, his fine and benevolent countenance was a perfect index of his mind, and his manners were courteous, frank and engaging. Brave, liberal and humane, devoted to his sovereign and loving his country with romantic fondness; in command so gentle and persuasive, yet so firm that he possessed the rare faculty of acquiring both the respect and the attachment of all who served under him. When urged by some friends shortly before his death to be more careful of his person, he replied, "how can I expect my men to go where I am afraid to lead them;" and although perhaps his anxiety ever to show a good example by being foremost in danger, induced him to expose himself more than strict prudence or formality warranted, yet if he erred on this point his error was that of a soldier. Elevated to the government of Upper Canada, he reclaimed many of the disaffected by mildness, and fixed the wavering by the argument of success, and having no national partialities to gratify, he meted equal favor and justice to all. British born subjects soon felt convinced that neither their religion or their birth-place was an obstacle to their advancement. Even over the minds of the Indians Sir Isaac Brock gained, at and after the capture of Detroit, an ascendancy altogether unexampled, and which he judiciously exercised for purposes conducive equally to the cause of humanity and to the interests of the country. He engaged them to throw aside the scalping knife, implanted in their breasts the virtues of clemency and forbearance, and taught them to feel pleasure and pride in the compassion extended to a vanquished enemy; in return they loved him as their common father, and while under his command were guilty of no excesses.*

In a despatch from Earl Bathurst, Secretary of State for the Colonies to Sir George Prevost, the following tribute of respect is paid by the British Government, to the memory of General Brock :—

"His Royal Highness the Prince Regent, is fully aware of the severe loss which His Majesty's service has experienced in the death of Major-General Sir Isaac Brock. That would have been sufficient to have clouded a victory of much greater importance. His Majesty has lost in him, not only an able and meritorious officer, but one who, in the exercise of his functions of Provincial Lieutenant-Governor of the Province, displayed qualities, admirably adapted to dismay the disloyal, to reconcile the wavering, and to animate the great mass of the inhabitants against successive attempts of the enemy to invade the Province, in the last of which he fell : too prodigal of that life of which his eminent services had taught us to understand the value."

But the gratitude of Great Britain did not end here. A public monument was decreed by the Imperial Government. It was voted in the House of Commons the 20th July, 1813, and was erected in St. Paul's Cathedral, the last resting-place of Nelson, Wellington, and other heroes and worthies, at a cost of £1,575 sterling. It is in the western ambulatory of the south transept, and was executed by Westmacott. A military monument on which are placed the sword and helmet of the deceased; a votive record supposed to have been raised by his companions to their lamented commander. His corpse reclines in the arms of a British soldier, whilst an Indian pays the tribute of regret his bravery and humanity elicited. Well do we remember how the crowds, returning from Cathedral service, lingered around, in admiration of this beautiful monument. The inscription is—

Erected at the Public Expense,

TO THE MEMORY OF

MAJOR–GENERAL SIR ISAAC BROCK,

Who gloriously fell on the 13th of October,

MDCCCXII.,

In resisting an attack on Queenston,

IN UPPER CANADA.

*Howison's " Sketches of Canada."

C

An Indian, "the chief of the band of the once great tribe of the Hurons visited England some time ago. I afterwards saw him in Quebec, and had a great deal of conversation with him. When asked what had struck him most of all that he had seen in England, he replied without hesitation, that it was the monument erected in St. Paul's to the memory of General Brock. It seemed to have impressed him with a high idea of the considerate beneficence of his great father, the King of England, that he not only had remembered the exploits and death of his white child, who had fallen beyond the big salt lake, but that he had even deigned to record on the marble sepulchre, the sorrows of the poor Indian weeping over his chief, untimely slain."*

And too, in consequence of an address from the Commons of Upper Canada to the Prince Regent, a munificent grant of 12,000 acres of land in this Province was bestowed on the four surviving brothers of Sir Isaac Brock, who in addition were allowed a pension of £200 a year for life by a vote of the Imperial Parliament.

And the gratitude of the people of Canada also took an equally enduring form. They desired to perpetuate the memory of the hero who had been the instrument of their deliverance, and they were not slow in executing their design; but whilst his noble deeds were still fresh in the memory of all, the Provincial Legislature erected a lofty column on the Queenston heights, near the spot where Brock fell.— The height of the monument from the base to the summit was 135 feet; and from the level of the Niagara River, which runs nearly under it, 485 feet. The monument was a Tuscan column on a rustic pedestal with a pedestal for a statue; the diameter of the base of the column was seventeen feet and a half, and the abacus of the capital was surmounted by an iron railing. The centre shaft containing the spiral staircase was ten feet in diameter. The inscription was nearly the same as is now seen on the present monument and will be given hereafter.

The remains of General Brock, and that of his gallant Aid-de-camp, Lieutenant-Colonel McDonell, were removed from Fort George, in solemn procession on the 13th October, 1824, and deposited in the resting place prepared for them in the monument.

Although twelve years had elapsed since the interment, the body of the general had undergone little change, his features being nearly per-

* DeRoo's Travels in North America in 1826.

fect and easily recognised, while that of Lieutenant Colonel McDonell was in a complete mass of decomposition.

The weather was remarkably fine, and before ten o'clock a very large concourse of people from all parts of the country had assembled on the plains of Niagara, in front of Fort George, in a bastion of which the bodies had been deposited for twelve years.

One hearse covered with black cloth and drawn by four black horses, each with a leader, contained both the bodies. Soon after ten, a line was formed by the 1st and 4th regiments of Lincoln Militia, with their right on the gate of Fort George, and their left extending along the road towards Queenston, the ranks being about forty paces from each other, within this line was formed a guard of honor of the 76th regiment in parade order, having its left on the Fort. As the hearse moved slowly from the Fort to the sound of solemn music, a detatchment of royal artillery began to fire the salute of nineteen guns, and the guard of honor presented arms.

On moving forward in ordinary time, the guard of honor broke into a column of eight divisions, with the right in front, and the procession took the following order :

A Staff Officer,

Subdivision of Grenadiers,

Band of Music,

Right wing of the 76th Regiment,

THE BODY,

Aide-de-camp to the late Major-General Sir Isaac Brock,

Chief Mourners,

Relatives of the late Colonel McDonell,

Commissioners for the Monument,

Heads of the Public Departments of the Civil Government,

Judges,

Members of the Executive Council,

His Excellency and Suite,

Left wing of the 76th Regiment,

Indian Chiefs of the Six Nations,

Officers of Militia not on duty, junior rank first forward, four deep,

Magistrates and Civilians,

With a long cavalcade of horsemen and carriages of every description.

The time occupied in moving from the Fort to Queenston, a distance of nearly seven miles, was about three hours. Being arrived opposite the spot where the lamented hero received his mortal wound, the whole procession halted and remained for a few minutes in solemn pause. It then ascended the heights, and to the spectator who had his station on the summit near the monument, nothing could be finer than the effect of the lengthened column winding slowly up the steep ascent in regular order, surrounded by scenery no where surpassed for romantic beauty. On the bodies being removed from the hearse and deposited in the vault, the guard of honor presented arms, whilst the artillery posted on the heights fired a salute of nineteen guns. The troops then marched in ordinary time round the monument, and immediately separated to their respective parades.

The remains of the brave McDonell lay to the left of those of the General. On the General's coffin, which is otherwise quite plain, and covered with black cloth, are two oval plates of silver, each six inches by four, one above the other. On the first is the following inscription :

Here lie the earthly remains of a brave and virtuous hero,
MAJOR–GENERAL SIR ISAAC BROCK,
Commander of the British forces and President administering the
Government of Upper Canada;
Who fell when gloriously engaging the enemies of his country,
at the head of the flank companies of the 49th regiment,
In the town of Queenstown,
On the morning of the 13th October, 1812,
Aged 42 years.
J. B. Glegg, A.D.C.

And on the second plate the following additional inscription is engraved:
The remains of the late
MAJOR–GENERAL SIR ISAAC BROCK, K.B.,
Removed from Fort George to this vault, on the 13th October, 1824.

Upon a similar plate on the lid of the Aide-de-Camp's coffin is engraved:
The remains of
LIEUTENANT COLONEL JOHN McDONELL,
Provincial Aid-de-Camp to the late
MAJOR GENERAL BROCK,
Who died on the 14th of October, 1812,
Of wounds received in action the day before,
Aged 25 years.

His Excellency the Lieutenant Governor, Major General Sir Peregrine Maitland, K.C.B., was in full dress—the two McDonells and Captain Dickinson of the 2nd Glengarry regiment, relatives of the deceased, Lieut. Colonel McDonell, in the Highland costume, appeared in the procession to great advantage, and seemed to excite much attention.

But amongst the assembled warriors and civilians none excited a more lively interest than the chiefs of the Six Nations Indians from the Grand River, whose warlike appearance, intrepid aspect, picturesque dress and ornaments, and majestic demeanour, accorded well with the solemn pomp and general character of a military procession ; among these young Brant, Bears Foot, and Henry, were distinguished.

Thus both Great Britain and Canada vied with each other in paying their tributes of respect and gratitude to the noble and the brave. The monument on Queenston Heights, was justly regarded by Canada with more affectionate veneration than any other structure in the Province ; and the feelings of indignation entertained by every one at the occurrence we are going to relate, may be easily conceived.

On Good Friday, the 17th April, 1840, a vagabond of the name of Lett, introduced a quantity of gunpowder into the monument with the fiendish purpose of destroying it, and the explosion effected by a train caused so much damage as to render the column altogether irreparable. Lett, who by birth was an Irishman and by settlement a Canadian,* had been compelled to fly into the United States for his share in the rebellion of 1837, and well knowing the feeling of attachment to the name and memory of General Brock which pervaded all classes of Canadians, he sought to gratify his malicious and vindictive spirit, and at the same time to wound and insult the people of Canada by this demon's deed. As may be imagined universal indignation was aroused, and a meeting was held on the 30th of July following, on Queenston Heights, for the purpose of adopting measures for the erection of another monument : the gallant Sir A. McNab, Bart., especially making the most stirring exertions to promote this great object. The gathering was attended by about 8000 persons, and the animation of the scene was increased by a detachment of Royal Artillery, who fired a salute, a detatchment of the 1st Dragoon Guards, with their bright helmets glittering in the sun, and the 93rd Regiment (Highlanders) in full costume.

Tupper's Life of Brock.

In Toronto the day was observed as a solemn holiday; the public offices were closed and all business was suspended, while thousands flocked from every part of the Province to testify their affection for the memory of one who, nearly thirty years before, had fallen in its defence. History, indeed, offers few parallels of such long cherished public attachment; steam vessels engaged for the occasion left their respective ports of Kingston, Cobourg, of Hamilton and Toronto, in time to arrive at the entrance of the Niagara river about ten o'clock in the forenoon. The whole of these, ten in number, then formed in line and ascended the river abreast with the Government steamer containing the Lieutenant-Governor Sir George Arthur and his Staff, leading the way. The British shore was lined with thousands, and the fleet of steamers filled with hundreds, each shouting and responding to the cheers of welcome from ship to shore, and from shore to ship again. The landing being effected, the march to the ground was accompanied by military guards and a fine military band. The public meeting was then held in the open air near the foot of the monument, and Sir George Arthur was in the chair. The Resolutions were moved and speeches made by some of the most eminent and most eloquent men holding high official stations in the Province. The speakers were His Excellency, Sir George Arthur, Chief Justice Sir J. B. Robinson, Bart., Mr. Justice Macaulay, Sir Allan McNab, Bart., David Thorburn, Esq., M. P., Colonel the Hon. W. Morris, Colonel R. D. Frazer, Colonel Clark, W. H. Merritt, Esq., M. P., Lieutenant-Colonel J. Baldwin, Lieutenant-Colonel Sherwood, Colonel Stanton, Colonel Kerby, Colonel the Hon. W. H. Draper, Colonel Angus McDonell, Hon. W. Sullivan, Lieutenant-Colonel Cartwright, Colonel Bostwick, Colonel McDougal, Hon. Mr. Justice Hagerman, Colonel Rutton, Lieutenant-Colonel Kearnes, Lieutenant-Colonel Kirkpatrick, H. J. Boulton, Esq., Lieutenant-Colonel Edward Thomson and Wm. Woodruff, Esq. And considering that amidst this grand and imposing assemblage there were a great number of veteran officers of the Canada militia, who had fought and bled with the lamented chief whose memory they were assembled to honor, and whose monument they had come to re-establish over his remains. The enthusiasm with which the whole mass was animated may readily be conceived, while the grand and picturesque contribution of natural objects of scenery beheld from the heights on which they were met, and the brightness of the day, added greatly to the effect of the whole.

There were altogether eleven Resolutions, of which the fifth was the following :

"*Resolved*,—That we recall to mind with admiration and gratitude, the perilous times in which Sir Isaac Brock led the small regular force, the loyal and gallant militia, and the brave and faithful Indian warriors to oppose the invaders. When his fortitude inspired courage and his sagacious policy gave confidence in despite of a hostile force apparently overwhelming."

In Major-General Sheaffe's despatch, already alluded to, mention is made of the great spirit with which Lieutenant Robinson led his men into action. The Lieutenant of that day is now the honored Chief Justice of Upper Canada ; on coming forward to move the fifth resolution he was received with the most enthusiastic cheers.

"If," he said, "it were intended by those who committed this shameful outrage, that the injury should be irreparable, the scene which is now before us, on these interesting heights, shows that they little understood the feelings of veneration for the memory of Brock which still dwells in the hearts of the people of Upper Canada. No man ever established a better claim to the affections of a country; and in re-calling the recollections of eight-and-twenty years, there is no difficulty in accounting for the feeling which has brought us together on this occasion. Among the many who are assembled here from all parts of this Province, I know there are some who saw as I did, with grief, the body of the lamented general borne from the field on which he fell, and many who witnessed with me the memorable scene of his interment in one of the bastions of Fort George. They can never, I am sure, forget the countenances of that gallant regiment which he had long commanded, when they saw deposited in the earth, the lamented officer, who had for so many years been their pride; they can never forget the feelings displayed by the loyal militia of this Province, when they were consigning to the grave the noble hero who had so lately achieved a glorious triumph in defence of his country; they looked forward to a dark and perilous future, and they felt that the earth was closing upon him, in whom more than in all other human means of defence, their confidence had been reposed. Nor can they forget the countenances, oppressed with grief, of those brave and faithful Indian warriors who admired and loved the gallant Brock ; who had bravely shared with him the dangers of that period, and who had most honorably distinguished themselves in the field when he closed his short but brilliant career.

It has, I know Sir, in the many years that have elapsed, been some-times objected, that General Brock's courage was greater than his prudence; that his attack of Fort Detroit, though it succeeded, was most likely to have failed, and was therefore injudicous, and that a similar rashness and want of cool calculation, were displayed in the manner of his death.

Those who lived in Upper Canada while these events were passing, can form a truer judgment; they know that what may to some seem rashness, was in fact prudence; unless indeed the defence of Canada was to be abandoned, in the almost desperate circumstances in which General Brock was placed. He had with him but a handful of men who had never been used to military discipline; few indeed that had ever seen actual service in the field; and he knew it must be some months before any considerable re-inforcement could be sent to him. He felt, therefore, that if he could not impress upon the enemy this truth, that wherever a Major-General of the British army, with but a few gallant soldiers of the line, and of the brave defenders of the soil, could be assembled against them, they must retire from the land which they had invaded, his cause was hopeless. If he had begun to compare numbers, and had reserved his small force in order to make a safer effort on a future day, then would thousands upon thou-sands of the people of the neighbouring States have been found pouring into the western portions of this Province; and when at last our mother country could send, as it was certain she would, her armies to our assist-ance, they would have had to expend their courage and their strength, in taking one strong position after another that had been erected by the enemy within our own territory.

And at the moment when the noble soldier fell, it is true, he fell in discharging a duty which might have been committed to a subordinate hand; true he might have reserved himself for a more deliberate and stronger effort; but he felt that hesitation might be ruin, that all de-pended upon his example of dauntless courage, of fearless self-devotion. Had it pleased Divine Providence to spare his invaluable life, who will say that his effort would have failed? It is true his gallant course was arrested by a fatal wound—such is the fortune of war; but the people of Canada did not feel that his precious life was therefore thrown away, deeply as they deplored his fall. In later periods of the contest, it some-times happened that the example of General Brock was not very closely followed. It was that cautious calculation which some supposed he wanted, which decided the day against us at Sackett's Harbour, it was the same cautious calculation which decided the day at Plattsburg; but no monuments have been erected to record the triumphs of those fields; it is not thus that trophies are won."

The Hon. Mr. Justice Macaulay, in moving the third resolution, thus elegantly expressed himself: "It was not my good fortune to serve in the field under the illustrious Brock, but I was under his command for a short period when commandant of the garrison of Quebec thirty years ago, and well remember his congratulating me upon receiving a commission in the army, accompanied with good wishes for my welfare, which I shall never forget. I feel myself an humble subaltern still, when called upon to address such an auditory and upon such a topic as the memory of Brock.— Looking at the animated mass covering these heights in 1840, to do further honor to the unfortunate victim of a war now old in history, one is prompted to ask, how it happens that the gallant General who has so long slept the sleep of death, left the lasting impression on the hearts of his countrymen which this scene exhibits; how comes it that the fame of Brock thus floats down the stream of time, broad, deep and fresh as the waters of the famed river with whose waters it might be almost said, his life's blood mingled? In reply, we might dwell upon his civil and military virtues, his patriotic self-devotion, his chivalrous gallantry, and his triumphant achievements. (Here one of the auditors added, 'and that he was an honest man'—an attribute most warmly responded to on every side—for an honest man is the noblest work of God.) Still it might be asked, what peculiar personal qualities predominated and gave him the talismanic influence and ascendancy over his fellow-men, which he acquired and wielded for his country's good? I answer, 'are there any seamen among you'? (Yes, yes, answered from the crowd.) Then I say it was the Nelsonian spirit that animated his breast, it was the mind instinctively to conceive, and the soul promptly to dare—incredible things to feeble hearts—with a skill and bearing which infused his chivalrous and enterprising spirit into all his followers, and impelled them energetically to realise whatever he boldly led the way to accomplish. It displayed itself too not only in the ranks of the disciplined soldiers, but in those also of the untrained militia of Upper Canada, as was amply proved on this memorable ground. Such were the shining and conspicuous qualities of the man that has rendered very dear his memory and his fame. Gentlemen, the resolution which I hold in my hand, is expressive of the indignation

D

felt throughout the Province, at the lawless act, the effect of which is visible before us."

After the resolutions had been carried by acclamation, and the public proceedings had terminated, 600 persons sat down to dinner in a temporary pavilion erected on the spot where the hero fell, Chief Justice Robinson presiding; and at this, as at the morning meeting, great eloquence was displayed in the speeches, great loyalty evinced in the feelings, and great enthusiasm prevailed. After the Queen's health had been drunk, the Chief Justice rose and said :

"I have now to propose the memory of the late gallant Sir Isaac Brock, of Colonel McDonell, and those who fell with them on Queenston Heights. That portion of you gentlemen, who were inhabitants of Upper Canada while General Brock served in its defence, are at no loss to account for the enthusiastic affection with which his memory is cherished among us. It was not merely on account of his intrepid courage and heroic firmness, neither was it solely because of his brillant success while he lived, nor because he so nobly laid down his life in our defence; it was, I think, that he united in his person, in a very remarkable degree, some qualities which are peculiarly calculated to attract the confidence and affection of mankind. There was in all he said and did that honesty of character which was so justly ascribed to him by a gentleman who proposed one of the resolutions. There was an inflexible integrity, uncommon energy and decision, which always inspire confidence and respect—a remarkable evenness in his whole demeanour of benevolence and firmness—a peculiarly commanding and soldier-like appearance—a generous, frank and manly bearing, and above all an entire devotion to his country. In short, I believe I shall best convey my own impression when I say, it would have required much more courage to refuse to follow General Brock, than to go with him wherever he would lead."

The meeting presented a proud display of high and noble feelings, honorable to the memory of the dead and equally so to the character of the living. It was conducted with great dignity and judgment, and no accident occurred to interrupt the pleasures of the day; the steam vessels re-embarking their passengers soon after sun-set and conveying back the individuals composing this congregated multitude to their respective homes in safety.*

---

*Buckingham's Canada.

The result of that meeting was the formation of a Building Committee for the erection of a new monument. It consisted of

Sir Allan Napier MacNab, Bart. M. P.,
Chief Justice Sir John Beverley Robinson, Bart.,
Hon. Mr. Justice Maclean,
Hon. Walter H. Dickson, M. L. C.,
Hon. Wm. Hamilton Merritt, M. P.,
Thomas Clark Street, Esq., M. P.,
Colonel James Kerby,
Colonel McDougal,
David Thorburn, Esq.,
Lieutenant Garrett, late 49th Regiment,
Colonel Robert Hamilton,
Captain H. Munro.

The first monument, as already stated, was erected by a grant from the Parliament of the Province. The present one by the voluntary contributions of the Militia and Indian Warriors of this Province; a grant from Parliament enabling the Committee to lay out the grounds and complete the outworks.

The operations were commenced in 1853, and on the 13th October in that year the ceremonies of laying the foundation stone and also the third re-interment of Brock took place. His remains and those of his Aide-de-Camp were temporarily removed from the ruined column to an adjoining burying ground, and were now to be conveyed to their resting place in the new structure. The day was splendidly fine, and a vast concourse attended to do homage to the illustrious dead. The pall-bearers were Cols. E. W. Thomson, W. Thompson, Duggan, Stanton, Kerby, Crooks, Zimmerman, Caron, Thorne, Servos, Clark, Wakefield and Miller. And among the chief mourners were Colonel Donald McDonell, Deputy Adjutant General for Canada East, Colonel Tachè, Lieut. Col. Irvine, and the survivors of 1812 and the brave Indian Chiefs.

The procession having gained the heights, the coffins were slowly—to the softened sounds of martial music—lowered down into their respective vaults, and deposited in the stone shells prepared for them.

The foundation stone was then laid by Lieut. Col. McDonell, brother of the gallant man who shared the fate and the honors of his Commander-in-Chief, and addresses were then delivered by the Hon. W. H. Merritt, M. P., David Thorburn, Esq., Col. Tachè, Col. E. W. Thomson, &c.

The column was completed in 1856. The surrounding grounds, containing about forty acres, have now been fenced in, a stone lodge erected with handsome wrought iron ornamental gates and cut stone piers, surmounted with the arms of the hero at the eastern entrance. From the entrance a carriage road, of easy ascent, winds up the steep, and is continued to the heights by an avenue 100 feet wide, planted with chesnuts, maples, &c., terminating at the monument in a circle 180 feet diameter.

The monument, as already stated, was designed by and completed under the superintendence of W. Thomas, Esq., architect of Toronto, who had also under his management and superintendence the erection of the lodge, laying out of the grounds, formation of roads, and all necessary works; and the manner in which he discharged these duties gave the committee great satisfaction.

Upon the solid rock is built a foundation 40 feet square and 10 feet thick of massive stone; upon this the structure stands in a grooved plinth or sub-basement 38 feet square and 27 feet in height, and has an eastern entrance by a massive oak door and bronze pateras, forming two galleries to the interior 114 feet in extent, round the inner pedestal, on the north and south sides of which, in vaults under the ground floor, are deposited the remains of General Brock, and those of his Aide-de-Camp, Colonel McDonell, in massive stone sarcophagi. On the exterior angles of the sub-basement are placed lions rampant seven feet in height, supporting shields with the armorial bearings of the hero—on the north side is the following inscription:

UPPER CANADA

Has dedicated this monument to the memory of the late

MAJOR-GENERAL SIR ISAAC BROCK, K.B.,

Provincial Lieut. Governor and Commander of the Forces in this Province, whose remains are deposited in the vault beneath.

Opposing the invading enemy, he fell in action near these heights,

On the 13th of October, 1812,

In the 43rd year of his age.

Revered and lamented by the people whom he governed, and deplored by the Sovereign to whose service his life had been devoted.

On brass plates, within the column, are the following inscriptions :

In a vault underneath are deposited the mortal remains
of the lamented

MAJOR–GENERAL SIR ISAAC BROCK, K.B.,

Who fell in action near these heights on 13th October, 1812,
And was entombed on the 16th October at the bastion of Fort George,
Niagara, removed from thence and re-interred under a monument to the
eastward of this site on the 13th October, 1824, and in consequence of that
monument having received irreparable injury by a lawless act on 17th
of April, 1840, it was found requisite to take down the former structure
and erect this monument—the foundation stone being laid, and the
remains again re-interred with due solemnity on 13th October, 1853.

In a vault beneath are deposited the mortal remains of

LIEUT. COL. JOHN McDONELL, P.A.D.C.,

And Aide-de-Camp to the lamented

MAJOR–GENERAL SIR ISAAC BROCK, K. B.,

Who fell mortally wounded in the battle of Queenston, on the 13th Oct.,
1812, and died on the following day.

His remains were removed and re-interred with due solemnity
On 13th October, 1853.

The column is placed on a platform slightly elevated, within a dwarf
wall enclosure 75.0 square, with a fosse around the interior.   At each
angle are placed massive military trophies, in pedestals, in carved stone,
20.0 in height.

Standing upon the sub-basement is the pedestal of the order, 16.9
square, and 38.0 in height, the die having on three of its enriched pan-
nelled sides, emblematic baso relievos, and on the north side, fronting
Queenston, the battle scene in alto relievo.

The plinth of the order is enriched with lion's heads, and wreaths in
bold relief.   The column is of the Roman composite order, 95.0 in height,
a fluted shaft, 10.0 diameter at the base ; the loftiest column known of
this style ; the lower tones enriched with laurel leaves, and the flutes
terminating on the base with palms.

The capital of the column is 16.0 square, and 12.6 high. On each face is sculptured a figure of victory, 10.6 high, with extended arms, grasping military shields as volutes; the acanthus leaves being wreathed with palms, the whole after the manner of the antique. From the ground to to the gallery at the top of the column, is continued a staircase of cut stone, worked with a solid nurel of 235 steps, and sufficiently lighted by loopholes in the fluting of the column, and other circular wreathed openings.

Upon the abacus stands the cippas, supporting the statue of the hero, sculptured in military costume, 17.0 high, the left hand resting on the sword, the right arm extended, with baton. The height from the ground to the top of the statue is 190, exceeding that of any monumental column, ancient or modern, known, with the exception of that on Fish Street Hill, London, England, by Sir Christopher Wren, architect, in commemoration of the great fire of 1666, 202 feet high, which exceeds it in height by 12 feet.

Great praise is due to the contractor, Mr. J. Worthington, for the skilful manner in which the work was executed; some of the pieces of stone in the formation of the capital of the column, being nearly three tons in weight, and elevated about 160 feet from the ground, and not the slightest accident occurring to any of the workmen during the period of its erection.

The comparative heights of some of the principal monuments of the kind, ancient and modern, are as follows :—

	ENTIRE HEIGHT.
Pompey's Pillar	90.0
Trojan's Pillar	115.0
Antonia Column	123.0
Monument on Fish Street Hill	202.0
York Column	137.0
Napoleon Column, Paris	132.0
July Column, Paris	156.0
Alexander Column, St. Petersburgh	175.6
Melville Column, Edinburgh	152.7
Nelson Column, Dublin	134.0
Nelson Column, Yarmouth	140.0
Nelson Column, London, from the level of the pavement in Trafalgar Square	171.0

Thus, then, there is only one column, either ancient or modern, in Europe, that exceeds the entire height of the Brock Monument, which is that erected in London by Sir Christopher Wren, in commemoration of the great fire in 1666.

From the top of the column, a magnificent view of the surrounding country can be obtained. To the north, and immediately below, is the Town of Queenston. It is at the head of the navigable waters of the Niagara. Queenston had used to be the place of depôt for all public stores and merchandise which were brought from Kingston and Lower Canada. Public stores for Forts Erie and Malden, and merchandise for all the country above, as well as the returns of furs and produce by that route downwards, were all stored for a time at Queenston. They were then transported over the carrying place, or portage, by waggons, a distance of nine miles to and from Chippawa, above the Falls. Railways have altered all this, and trade has been diverted into other channels. The principal buildings were burnt during the war.

In the distance, about seven miles, is the Town of Niagara, a place of much business and resort. It is situate at the mouth of the Niagara River. As you enter the town from Queenston, is the old Fort George ; about a mile north of the town is Fort Missessaga. On the American side, opposite, is Fort Niagara.

On the east of the monument, is Lewiston, and the beautiful Suspension Bridge. From the sudden change in the face of the country at this spot, and the equally sudden change in the river, with respect to its breadth, depth, and current, it has been conjectured that the Falls, somewhere about thirty thousand years ago, must have been at this place where the waves are so abruptly contracted between the hills ; and the conjecture is strengthened by the fact well ascertained, that the Falls have receded very considerably since they were first visited by Europeans, and that they are still receding every year.

To the south are the beautiful villages of Stamford, Drummondville, and the battle field of Lundy's Lane, and a little to the left is the terrific whirlpool, almost as tremendous as the Mælstrom of Norway.

The view from this monument of the surrounding country, is perhaps unsurpassed for magnificence by any on the American continent, and the spot has been appropriately chosen as the fittest to blazon forth the achievements of the virtuous and the brave.

> As Fame alighted on the mountain's crest,
> She loudly blew her trumpet's mighty blast,
> Ere she repeated victory's notes, she cast
> A look around and stopped : of power bereft,
> Her bosom heaved, her breath she drew with pain,
> Her favorite BROCK lay slaughtered on the plain !
> Glory threw on his grave a laurel wreath,
> And Fame proclaims, " A hero sleeps beneath."

William Brock, the grandfather of our hero, was connected by marriage with one of the principal and most eminent families of the island of Guernsey. He had three sons and a daughter.

John Brock, Esq., his second son, had by his wife Elizabeth De Lesle, a very numerous family of ten sons and four daughters, of whom eight sons and two daughters reached maturity. He died in June, 1777, at Dinan, in Brittany, where he had gone for the benefit of the waters, at the early age of 48 years. In his youth he was a midshipman in the navy, and in that capacity had made a voyage to India, which was then considered a great undertaking. The family was left in independent if not in affluent circumstances.

Isaac Brock, the eighth son, was born in the parish of St. Peter-Port, Guernsey, on the 6th October, 1769, the year which gave birth to Napoleon and Wellington. In his boyhood he was like his brothers, unusually tall, robust and precocious, and with an appearance much beyond his age, remarkable chiefly for his extreme gentleness. In his eleventh year he was sent to school at Southampton, and his education was concluded by his being placed for a twelve month under a French protestant clergyman at Rotterdam, for the purpose of learning the French language. The eldest brother John, a lieutenant in the 8th (the King's Regiment) being promoted to a company by purchase, Isaac succeeded, also by purchase, to the ensigncy which consequently became vacant in that regiment, and to which he was appointed on 2nd March, 1785, soon after he had completed his 15th year. In 1790 he was promoted to a lieutenancy and was quartered in Guernsey and Jersey. At the close of that year he obtained an independent company. He exchanged soon after into the 49th, which regiment he joined at Barbadoes in 1791, and he remained doing duty there and afterwards in Jamaica until 1793, when he was compelled to return very suddenly to England on sick leave. On his return from Jamaica Captain Brock was employed on the recruiting service in England

and afterwards in charge of a number of recruits in Jersey. On 24th of June, 1795, he purchased his majority. On 27th of October, 1797, just after he had completed his twenty-eighth year, Major Brock purchased his lieutenant-colonelcy, and soon after became senior lieutenant-colonel of the 49th. In 1799 his regiment embarked on an expedition under Sir Ralph Abercrombie to Holland, then in alliance with the French republic. On its landing an engagement took place which cost the British about 1000 men. During this campaign Lieutenant-Colonel Brock distinguished himself in command of his regiment, and on the 2nd October, in the battle of Egmont-op-Zee, was slightly wounded.

The 49th, on the return of the expedition from Holland, was again quartered in Jersey, and early in 1801 was embarked in the fleet destined for the Baltic under Sir Hyde Parker, and Lieutenant-Colonel Brock was the second in command of the land forces at the memorable attack of Copenhagen by Lord Nelson, on the 2nd of April. On the return of the 49th to England it was collected at Colchester, and in the Spring following, 1802, the regiment sailed for Canada, the scene of the fame and death of its commanding officer.

In less than eighteen months after the arrival of the 49th in Canada, a serious conspiracy was on the point of breaking out in that part of the regiment which was in garrison at Fort George. The officer in command, had, it seems, more by useless annoyance than actual severity, exasperated the men to that degree, that they formed a plot to murder all the officers present with the exception of a young man who had recently joined, and then to cross over to the United States. Lieutenant-Colonel Brock, by promptitude of action, secured the ringleaders; and four, on being tried by Court Martial, were condemned to suffer death, and were shot at Quebec in the presence of the garrison, early in March, 1804. The unfortunate sufferers declared publicly that had they continued under the command of Colonel Brock, they would have escaped their melancholy end, and as may be easily conceived, he felt no little anguish that they who had so recently and so bravely fought under him in Holland and at Copenhagen, were thus doomed to end their lives the victims of unruly passions, inflamed by vexatious authority. He was now directed to assume the command at Fort George, and all complaint and desertion instantly ceased. The Duke of York was heard to declare that Lieut-Colonel Brock, from one of the worst, had made the 49th one of the best regiments in the service.

E

In the fall of 1805—in October of which year he was made full Colonel —Colonel Brock returned to Europe on leave; and early in the following year he laid before his Royal Highness the Commander-in-Chief the outlines of a plan for the formation of a veteran battalion to serve in the Canadas, and for which he received the special thanks of the Duke of York.

While on a visit to his family and friends in Guernsey, Colonel Brock deemed the intelligence from the United States to be of so warlike a character that he resolved on returning to Canada. He left London on the 26th June, 1806, and hurried away from Europe, never to return.

Soon after his arrival in Canada, Colonel Brock succeeded on the 27th September, 1806, to the command of the troops in the two Provinces, making Quebec his residence; Colonel Bowes—afterwards slain on the 27th June, 1812, while leading the troops to the assault of the forts of Salamanca—having resigned that command on his departure for England. On the 2d July, 1808, Colonel Brock was appointed to act as a Brigadier; a distinguished mark of approval of his conduct.

Brigadier Brock, in 1810, proceeded to the Upper Province, having been replaced at Quebec by Baron de Rottenburg, and he continued in command of the troops there till his death; Lieutenant-Governor Gore at that time administering the civil Government.

On the 4th June, 1811, Brigadier Brock was promoted and appointed by the Prince Regent, to serve as a Major-General on the staff of North America.

Sir James Craig, who had been in chief command of the British North American Provinces, embarked for England in June, 1811, in ill health, and died several months after his arrival there. He was succeeded by Sir George Prevost, who arrived at Quebec in September; and on the 9th of October Major-General Brock, in addition to the command of the troops, was appointed President and Administrator of the Government in Upper Canada, in place of Lieutenant-Governor Gore, who returned to England, on leave. At the close of the year, His Royal Highness the Duke of York expressed at length every inclination to gratify Major-General Brock's wishes for more active employment in Europe, and Sir Geo. Prevost was authorised to replace him by another officer; but when the permission reached Canada early in 1812, a war with the United States was evidently near at hand, and Major-General Brock, with such a prospect, was retained both by honor and inclination in the country, and he employed himself vigorously to the adoption of such precautionary measures as he deemed necessary to meet all future contingencies. From the first moment of being placed at the head of the Government, he appears to have been convinced that war was inevitable, and in consequence used every exertion to place the Province in as respectable a state of defence as his very limited means would admit. Immediately after war was declared, he made Fort George his head quarters, and superintended the various defences on the river. He then went to York, (now Toronto) where the Legislature was assembled, and having despatched the public business, set out for Amherstburg on the 6th of August, with 250 militia, who cheerfully came forward to accompany him. The taking of Detroit soon followed, an achievement which his energy and decision crowned with such unqualified success, that the Government at home appointed him an extra Knight of the most Honorable Order of the Bath, and he was gazetted to this mark of his country's approbation, so gratifying to the feelings of a soldier, on the 10th October, but he lived not long enough to learn that he had obtained so honorable a distinction, the knowledge of which would have cheered him in his last moments. On the 6th October when his despatches, accompanied by the colors of the U. S. 4th regiment, reached London, the Park and Tower guns fired a salute, and in one short week afterwards Brock died.

> Low bending o'er the rugged bier,
> The soldier drops the mournful tear,
> For life departed, valour driven,
> Fresh from the field of death to heaven.
>
> But time shall fondly trace the name
> Of BROCK upon the scrolls of fame,
> And those bright laurels, which should wave
> Upon the brow of one so brave,
> Shall flourish vernal o'er his grave.